AF324767

I would blast off into space . . .

...and travel past the moon.

I would land on a distant planet…

…where I might bump into a
strange creature

with a wiggly-woggly trunk and two
sharp horns...

...who lived in a wiggly-woggly house

and ate wiggly-woggly food.

Then I might find a hidden city...

...by a purple lake under a pink moon.

I might come across a space garden

with stripy flowers and a tree
of stars.

And I would put some in my pocket...

...and take them home to Mom.